Dinosaur School

DINOSAURS HELP OUT

Please visit our website, www.garethstevens.com. For a free color catalog of all our high-quality books, call toll free 1-800-542-2595 or fax 1-877-542-2596.

Library of Congress Cataloging-in-Publication Data

Appleby, Alex.
Dinosaurs help out / by Alex Appleby.
   p. cm. — (Dinosaur school)
ISBN 978-1-4339-9054-0 (pbk.)
ISBN 978-1-4339-9055-7 (6-pack)
ISBN 978-1-4339-9053-3 (library binding)
1. Helping behavior—Juvenile literature. I. Appleby, Alex. II. Title.
TX871.A66 2014
642.7—dc23

First Edition

Published in 2014 by
Gareth Stevens Publishing
111 East 14th Street, Suite 349
New York, NY 10003

Designer: Andrea Davison-Bartolotta
Editor: Ryan Nagelhout

All illustrations by Planman Technologies

Printed in the United States of America

CPSIA compliance information: Batch #CS13GS: For further information contact Gareth Stevens, New York, New York at 1-800-542-2595.

DINOSAURS HELP OUT

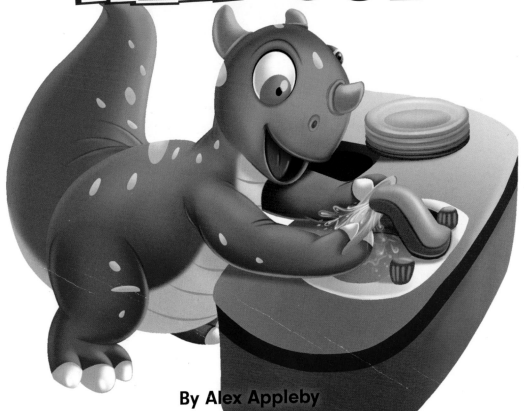

By Alex Appleby

Gareth Stevens
Publishing

I help my mom.

I clean my room.

I help my dad.

I rake the leaves.

I help my brother.

I find his hat.

I help my sister.

I find her doll.

I help my grandma.

I water her plants.

I help my grandpa.

I walk his dog.

I help my teacher.

I sweep the floor.

I help my neighbor.

I shovel the snow.

I help my town.

I pick up trash.

I help my friend.

We bake cookies!

Dinosaurs Help Out

baking cookies

finding a hat

sweeping the floor

cleaning a room

raking leaves

walking a dog

finding a doll

shoveling snow

watering plants